WHEN TWO WORLDS COLLIDE

Linny Roberts (L.T.R)

ISBN-13: 9798544336594
ISBN-10: 1477123456

Cover design by: Art Painter
Library of Congress Control Number: 2018675309
Printed in the United States of America

Every book i write is dedicated to my wife, the one woman who always stands by my side and helps me throughout any journey i decide to take, she will always be my hero.

I also want to dedicate this book to these two special people i had the pleasure to meet in my life.

Trevor Revell (Gramps-Our Hero) one of the greatest men to ever walk this earth. A man full of courage and Dignity.

Jade-Leigh one of the strongest women i know, no matter what life throws at her she is full of courage and strength.

They really are true life hero's.

A s I sat dazing out of the bedroom window, my mind and thoughts are elsewhere. I often spend my time looking up at the big green hills surrounding my house, through the summer months the view is crystal clear with the sun shining over them, through the winter months its very picturesque with a full blanket of snow. I truly live in a beautiful place. My mum and dad bought this house when I was a little girl, I remember first moving here- I thought we had moved into a castle, we have 3 reception rooms, a best room as my dad likes to call it. No children are allowed in this room, it's where dad has all his important meetings. The big black double wooden doors are always locked. The kitchen is very large with an island in the middle. Filled with white cupboards all around with neon blue under counter lights. Mom always likes to entertain in this room on the rare occasion of her not working. 5 bedrooms, 3 bathrooms. The house was decorated in light grey, with glass sideboards with diamond chandlers hanging from every ceiling. There was an open glass staircase leading to the upstairs and an exceptionally large garden, this is where I spent most of my time. The garden is filled with all sorts of chairs up on the decking, swimming pool, tennis court- everything a child could ever want, but not everything is as it seems. I have an elder sister who never wants to pay me any attention, she's either working or out partying. She works as a nurse, so I guess she deserve to let her hair down. mom is always touring being a stage manager we never see her, and dad always has meetings going on, and me, well I'm just Lou.

CHAPTER ONE

14 years ago

I am in high school now. My middle school days are finally behind me. All my years in school have been hard. You could almost say traumatic. I am not the same as the other children. I am different in so many ways, I don't connect like they do in anything. I'm a dreamer, I don't have an interest in anything they are doing. I like to keep myself to myself, I know I'm different and I feel things differently. I know I look the same as everyone else- I just don't think the same as everyone. Nothing really made sense to me until last year when i turned 13. So, let me take you back to the beginning.

I was born to my parents Shelly and David in June, 14 years ago. My sister Nicole was already 5 years old when I came along. I was born through a huge thunderstorm; Mom had taken 6 months leave from work while dad carried on. Nothing seemed out of the ordinary when I was growing up, mom just said I was very clever for my age. They put it down to having a good nanny. Mom went back to work while I was still young, so my Nanny Megan basically brought me up. In fact, she only stopped looking after me two years ago, I'm still close to her and we ring each other at least once a day. At the age of two I could count, write, do the alphabet, spell I could do most things way before I was supposed to. I don't remember the first house we lived in, but we moved into this house when I was three. The first time I came in I remember asking mom if I was a princess to live here and she just smiled at me. Mom had just had a promotion so we could afford something bigger, that's when I remember starting to miss her. She would go to work on a Monday morning and not come back for what seemed like weeks. I've since learnt she only worked away for a few days but to a three-year-old it doesn't seem that way. It wasn't until I got a bit older, she would work for weeks on end away.

I quickly settled into the new surroundings and started exploring the new house. One of the reception rooms was done out to be the children's room, filled with toys, books, colourings but my favourite was the dolls house. I would play for hours with it, while Megan cleaned the house. I never really knew, and still don't what dad's job really was, Mom just said not to bother him when he had the men from work around. So, me and Megan would spend the days together once she was done cleaning. We either played in the garden or she would take me out food shopping with her. It was here that she realised there was something special within me. To Megan's disbelief I would total all the shopping up before we even got to the till, and I was never wrong on the amount. She knew I was too clever for my own good. She argued with Mom to let her home school me. She said I was too clever for mainstream school, but mom was adamant I was to go. She said I would grow up with social problems so off to nursery I went. With my birthday being in June I started two months after my third birthday.

It wasn't long before the school had called my mom in for a meeting, due to her hectic work schedule- Megan ended up going to hear the teacher's concern about my lack of interaction with the other children. How I would keep myself in one corner of the room, away from everyone else they were concerned. I didn't speak, they believed I hadn't met the standards of socialising before I came to nursery. I hadn't developed in the right time frame and wanted me to see a specialist. Megan knew something wasn't right, the child who can count a full trolley load, who can hold an adult conversation at three. She tried to get to the bottom of my problems, but I never answered her. I completed my journey with the specialist, and she couldn't solve the problem either. So, I was left to my own devices. I didn't learn much at nursery as I already knew it, I did start to play with the other children and eventually made a few friends, one of which- Grace. Me and Grace have gone through all our school years, she's stood by me through it all. Although she doesn't know the full story but of what she does, she's been a true best friend. I finished nursery and only then did I notice more of what was happening, I began to see how clever I was compared to my age group and the fact I could do things no-one else could. Nevertheless, I tried to fit in with everyone and tried to act normal. I settled into school and home life. By the time I was 7, Mom was out touring for weeks sometimes months, Megan had moved into our family home while dad was working. Megan tried to make school holidays fun and took me out either to the theme park, leisure parks or safaris anywhere that was out the house and fun to do. Life was good I had dealt with the fact I was different and just got on with it. The main factor for me was I was here and for whatever reason I was given ability's that no-one else had.

CHAPTER 2

Theme Park disaster

I t was the last week of the school holidays and Megan decided to take me to a theme park, Nicole had not long turned 13 and was more interested in spending time with her mates doing whatever teenagers did. So, it just ended up being me and Megan. Theme parks were my favourite places to go. I was even more excited this time round because I was old enough to actually go on the bigger rides. I was taller than average for an 8-year-old, my build was tall and thin with long blonde curly hair, pale blue eyes and I always wore skinny jeans and a t-shirt, I either wore sliders or trainers depending on the weather. This particular day was sunny and hot, being the end of August, it was a glorious day. So, you guessed right I wore my favourite white t-shirt with my black skinny ripped jeans and a pair of sliders. Megan wore her blue dress with a pair of white sandals. Packed with our picnic in the boot we set off.

The theme park was over an hour away, but we sang along to all the recent song releases. Megan was a young nanny she was only in her 20's so she listened to all the newest songs. Mom and dad had me late on in their marriage. Mom was early 40s and dad was already mid-way through his when I came along, so they weren't really down with the kids so to speak. I think this is why me and Megan got on and get on so well now. We finally arrived at the theme park, I could hear the rush and excitement in all the children as they walked along the path to the entrance. The path was pretty long filled with trees two meters apart all the way up, running symmetrically. I had never been to this park, Megan had picked it for this simple fact, and an added bonus of the fact it was known for its thrill in big rides. We finished the walk up the path just to be met with a huge queue of people waiting to enter the park. Before you even entered the actual park gate's you were taken in style by a mid-air train. We queued for about half an hour before we got to the platform of the train. It screeched to a halt, and we were next. As the train arrived every carriage was covered in different picture's advertising something. One carriage had the M & M's all over it brightly coloured yellow and blue, the next was blue with a huge Pepsi can, then there was a red carriage with a coke can on and the last one was silver with a huge tiger, polar bear, and a lion on. This theme park had a theme of dressed up characters roaming around. You could have pictures with them as a key ring and printed out. We started walking towards the locked gate ready for them to open for us. I was secretly praying we would get the characters carriage. We ended up with the M & M's carriage, I didn't mind it was colourful. There were 10 to a carriage, sat next to me was a young lad and his mom, Megan sat opposite me. We set off slowly from the station, I stared out the window so happy to be here and so happy mom had picked Megan to be my nanny, it could have been a lot worse with an older nanny who liked to stay at home doing chores the whole time. The train took you on a tour of the park so you could see all the rides available to go on, all the activities you could do and all the places you could eat at. Unable to hold my excitement in I turned to Megan with a massive grin on my face, she too was beaming with happiness, for the simple fact I was. The train took around 15 minutes to get to the other side. We began walking off the train hand in hand down the long-curved slope towards the ground floor. As you got down out of the tunnel, there were three massive statues of the tiger, polar bear, and lion. They stood 15 feet tall, Megan took a picture of us stood next to them, then we made our way to the main entrance. There was a small queue in front of us but nothing bad, we went through the turn style entrance before we knew it. As soon as we entered i just remember looking up at the huge roller coasters standing tall in the background, all had hoops and turns, big drops. Eager to ride my first roller-coaster I ran a few meters in front. Turning around every few seconds to check Megan was still behind me. I reached the fountain in the middle of the path, it was a big and round made out of grey concrete, in the middle made out of stone were the words welcome to Thrill Seekers. I sat on the edge waiting for Megan to catch up looking deep into the water. Right at the bottom were loads of sunken pennies. Just as I turned around out appeared a man, wearing a round black cowboy hat, long black coat with trousers and a woolly jumper, his shoes were pointed shinny and black and he was wearing leather gloves. A-bit odd for a hot summers day I thought to myself. He walked towards me.

"Throw one in girl, it brings you luck" he said in a stern rough voice.

I just looked at him, speechless in how different he looked to everyone else. He raised one hand and gave his hat a tug with half a smile walking straight pass me. Without warning he disappeared. Megan had finally caught up. Looking very puzzled I looked down towards the pennies in the fountain. There must have been a couple of hundred just lying there.

"Have you got a penny" I asked Megan.

"Yeah, what for" Megan replied confused.

"To throw into the bottom of here, it brings you luck, that man said so" I smiled back. Megan looking around.

"What man?" She replied

"The man just talking to me" I said confused. Megan looked at me like she had no idea what I was talking about.

"Lou, you've been sat here on your own the whole time I could see you from up there" Megan said worried. I lent to my right to look around Megan to see this man again, but he was no-where to be seen in the crowd of people, surely, he would stick out like a sore thumb I thought to myself.

"You didn't see that man with the cowboy hat, wearing all black?" I asked. I stood up looking frantically at Megan for her answer.

"No Lou you were on your own"

Maybe I was daydreaming, or it was something I imagined, I didn't know but nothing was going to spoil my day, so I tossed my penny into the fountain, and we began our day.

First, we went on the ghost train, it started outside then worked its way through staged rooms. Each one was through a set of black doors that the train opened. It was two to a cart so me and Megan were together, she was secretly more scared than I was, she was holding my hand so tight through the dark rooms, she even let out a scream now and again when something dropped in front of us. Next, we went on the turning teacups, these were inside- only the front of the room was open, they had disco lights that changed to the rhythm of the music. They spun around so fast we both felt sick when we came off them. To give us some fresh air we decided to walk around the open market to get some souvenirs for the family. We brought Mom a new pen it was orange with the name Rory on in name of the tiger- she was forever losing hers, Dad we got a new clip board his had seen better days and Nicole we got a big bag of sweets, she had a very sweet tooth. By this time, it was time for our picnic. We picked a patch near the entrance to the big rollercoaster; this was our next point of call. We lay the blanket out on the floor, and we began to get our food out. Ham muffins, cheese muffins, sausage rolls, crisp, chocolate all my favourite things. We were starving so it didn't take long for us to demolish everything and end up with full bellies. We decided to lay down to let our food settle and catch a-bit of the sun. Just as I started to lay down, I had a really strange feeling, I began to feel clammy. A rush of sickness appeared over me and a sharp pain in the left side of my face, my legs started to kick uncontrollably in the air.

"Are you ok?" Megan asked worried.

I just looked at her, I knew she had asked me something, but it didn't register, it went in one ear straight out of the other. She asked again but her voice slowly started to fade by the sound of people screaming.

"What's all the screaming about?" I shouted to Megan

"Are you ok Lou, why are you shouting I'm right next to you, no-one Is screaming" she replied. I could barely hear her still.

I pushed my head back and closed my eyes, trying to drown the sound of screams out. My head started to twitch from side to side when this high-pitched screaming started. I saw something really bad; I could see everyone running out of the roller coaster entrance shouting and screaming – they needed help, all of them. My eyes then took me deeper into the rollercoaster part of the theme park, under the arched entrance and round the corner, on both sides were the two main coasters. One side was the red one and the other side was the yellow one. The yellow one was still going around the track, but as I turned to the red one it was awfully quiet, the carriage was no-where to be seen. I started walking towards the rollercoaster and right down the bottom, there it was the carriage had fell of the track and was upside down on the floor. The people were still strapped inside- they were stuck.

I rushed over to the carriage shouting "is everyone ok?" I had no response. I could hear them screaming out in pain.

"Is anyone seriously hurt?" I began to ask.

"No-one is coming- they don't know we have crashed" I heard one say

"Help is anyone out there?" Another shouted

"Guys I'm here is anyone seriously hurt" I asked again. Then it suddenly dawned on me they couldn't hear me. I need to get back; they can't see me I shouted to myself. My head fell forwards and my eyes opened- everything was calm.

Megan was stroking my leg she begins to talk worried.

"Lou, are you ok, you were shaking making funny noises"

"We need to go there's been an accident" I replied rushing up to my feet, heading towards the rollercoaster entrance.

As we rushed our way to the entrance, I looked around me and realised no-one was rushing around, no-one was screaming or running towards the exit.

"What are you talking about Lou" Megan shouts trying to keep up.

"I've just seen it, the red rollercoaster its upside down-people are trapped" I frantically replied. We walked past the walk around haunted castle. People were queued outside carrying on as normal, laughing and joking, scaring each other before they went in. We reached the corner.

"Wait up, Lou I can't keep up "Megan trying to catch her breath.

I turned to face the two rollercoaster's the yellow doing its normal routine around the track, the red had just pulled out of the start.

"See, nothing to worry about" Megan smiled to me.

What is happening to me I thought to myself, first a man no-one else had seen and now this.

"I saw it- I really did they were upside down, over there. Right at the end" I pointed with a shaky hand.

I started to watch the red rollercoaster go round the track, it was climbing up the hill, ready to do the drop, it whizzes down the drop tossing and turning all the turns, then it starts to do the hoop.

"It's not going to make it" I shouted turning to Megan.

I could see the rollercoaster had lost its speed. It got half-way round the hoop, when all of a sudden it stopped right at the top. It shot backwards going the wrong way around the track, it was just about to do a right hand 90 degree turn when a loud bang shattered the whole theme park. Me and Megan dropped to our knee's covering our ears. There was a high-pitched scream when everything fell silent. We slowly stood up to see people rushing around screaming running towards the exit. I turned to face the carriage- which was upside down with the riders trapped inside. Without saying a word Megan slightly gripping my shoulders began to ask

"But, what, how did you know"

We rushed over to aid the injured.

"Is everyone ok?" Megan shouts

"My legs" one screams

"I'm hurting" another one screams.

We comforted them as much as we could before the emergency services came, they had raised the alarm, we could hear it all over the park. This high-pitched siren pierced everyone's ears.

"Clear the area" a man shouted through a microphone.

"Come on, Lou we will wait over here" Megan says guiding me to the grass bank top to the left of the carriage.

We sat on the grass verge watching the emergency service cut everyone free. There were ambulances everywhere, air ambulances, fire fighters, police. It was a scene of madness. Absolute chaos I looked at Megan she was sat their pale as a ghost, she was just staring. I placed my hand on her knee. You could hear everyone cry out in pain as they were carried out on stretchers.

"Please, don't ask me I just don't know" I pleaded with her. Megan just looked at me. I knew her mind was full of questions.

"I had better send a picture to your mom, she will hear about this on the news, she will want to know you're ok" Before warning a flash of light went straight through my eyes as she took the picture.

"You will need to move under the tree, I can't see you with all the flashing blue lights" she asks.

I moved under the tree; it was pretty shielded here. No-one

or nothing but trees around me. She took the picture.
Megan was pale with bearded eyes screams dropping the phone.
"What's wrong" I screamed back.
Megan lent to the left to look straight through me.
"Come here" she cried
She showed me the picture, I couldn't believe what I was seeing, stood behind me, almost transparent was a man. The cowboy man that no-one else could see but me. We searched frantically for the cowboy, but he was no-where to be seen.

CHAPTER 3

The Girl

After the theme park I tried to act as normal as possible, Megan and I never spoke of it. I told her I didn't know how and what was happening, and she respected my decision. She obviously didn't tell Mom and Dad; they main concern was that we weren't hurt in it all. So, it was our secret. I went back to school, and everything was fine for a few months, I was a normal child for the time being, me and Grace would play nicely together. I thought nothing could spoil the way I felt at this exact moment. We were getting along. Then without any warning a new girl started, Tracey, she started halfway through the school year so Grace being the kind-hearted girl she was, took Tracey under her wing. They instantly hit it off and I felt like I was being left out and losing my best friend. They would always play together, when it was paired tasks, Tracey would always choose Grace to pair off with, so I was left alone, I was always paired with the boy no one else wanted to be with. It wasn't all bad he was actually funny, it's just not a nice feeling when it's almost been just the two of us.

Grace was small built and quite plump, she had long straight hair and always wore dresses, she was basically the complete opposite to me, but for some reason we were best friends and our friendship always worked out regardless of who or what would come in our way. Although something felt different this time. I actually thought someone could get in the way of us. That someone being Tracey. Although Tracey seemed nice enough, I didn't want to give her my time to find out for myself, I had an instant dislike from the start. At break times they did always try to involve me, but I would rather huff about it, and I began to draw myself in once again. Grace had built my confidence up without her even knowing she had done so, I started coming out of my shell when we were friends and once felt invincible. Now being alone again I was quiet, and I didn't want to speak to anyone. I spent my break times walking the fields of the school, avoiding anyone who came into contact with me. I often looked out onto the playground at all the other children playing together wondering why I couldn't just fit in, wishing I could be more like them, but I had no confidence at all without Grace being around me. Grace picked up on my mood swings and this put a wedge between us, so we weren't close at all. On this particular day, I was hiding behind the tallest tree in the school grounds. Hoping no one could see me. I was listening to the birds tweeting their songs, minding my own business, when in the background I could see a figure, this figure wasn't particularly big and seemed to be hunched over as if they were in pain. I really didn't want to take a closer look, but my head was telling me I needed to.

Slowly walking over to the other side of the field, looking around me to make sure no one had spotted me, I began to get closer. The closer I got the more anxious I became. There were only a couple of trees between us when I finally spotted it was a young girl, probably a similar age to me. She had her back to me. She was slightly hunched over and wearing unusual clothing. Nothing like my clothes. She had a long coat on, it looked like it was made out of leather. She had strange boots that were ripped in several places. When I finally reached the young girl, she still had her back towards me. Nervous who she was, I began to feel unwell, an un-easy feeling appeared over me. I hadn't felt this way for some time.

"Are you ok?" I asked shaking.

The girl didn't move an inch, stood as still as a statue.

"Excuse me- can you hear me" I patiently asked. But still the girl didn't move, in the distance I heard the break time bell ringing.

"My breaks over now-"I said quietly hoping the girl would give me some indication she had heard me, but still no response. I slowly moved to the right, trying to catch a glimpse of the girl. Her long black hair covered the side of her face so I couldn't see anything. Unsure what to do next, I reached my hand out, within inches of her hair when a familiar voice shout,

"Louise come on dear time to go in".

I turned to face Mrs Vape stood behind with a nod of the head, I quickly turned back around. The girl had gone. Extremely puzzled I ran towards Mrs Vape.

"What are you doing out in this field on your own Louise" she questioned "its too far out from the school to be alone" she continued Not wanting to mention anything I just looked up and smiled.

My next lesson was English, I usually sat next to Grace, but we weren't really getting on so without confusing the situation anymore I decided to sit at the table next to the teacher. Still in total shock after my break time incident I didn't want to draw any more attention to me than there needed to be. The lesson went quickly and before I knew it, it was lunch time. As my new normal routine, I was sat alone eating my packed lunch Megan had made me. Full to the top with all my favourite things as always, but there was one thing on my mind-the girl. The rule for lunch time in this school was no one was allowed outside until they had eaten their lunch, so I rushed down my sandwich eager to get back out. Grace and Tracey sat at the table behind me, laughing and giggling together I tried to ignore their comments.

"Look at her it's like she's never eaten before" Grace remarks "All the money her mom has, you would think she would eat like the queen" Tracey replies.

I thought to myself what have I done so badly to these girls to make them act the way they were.

Trying not to retaliate I ignored them both. Finished off my lunch and made my way out through the corridor. The dining hall was the opposite side of the school, there were quite a few left and right turns through the long narrow corridor, each one a different colour as you reached different year groups. Year 6 was the closest to the dining hall, descending through to year 1 closest to the playground. I reached year one and opened the big blue half glass doors out to the playground. I stopped for a second looking around, listening to the children running around, screaming, laughing, playing tag, some were doing dance competitions, others were playing football letting some steam off. But me, I was heading one place and one place only- the fields. I dodged my way through the football game, up the steps till I reached the green gate which separated the playground to the field. The field was usually locked for pupils unless it was really sunny, it was only really used for sports day, but the gate had been open for a few days now. I walked through towards the tall tree again, impatient to see if the girl was around. I looked left then right, straight ahead and then turned back around but she was nowhere to be seen. The field must have been around 3 football pitches in size, the outskirts had trees all around, each spaced about 2 meters apart. In the middle of it had a running track painted with white lines and each side had two goal posts both with a white box painted on. I sat under the tree for the rest of the lunch time, but she never appeared.

I remembered going home that afternoon, unusually quieter than normal. Megan knowing me all too well she began with the questions.

"Are you ok? You seem a little quiet" she asked.

Deciding whether to go down that path again or not was a hard decision but at the time, I didn't want to worry Megan. It had only just been a couple of months since the theme park, so I did what I did best and hid it.

"Just tired" I replied sharply

Megan knew that meant I don't want to talk, and she left me be.

The next day started the same as every other day, me getting up late, Megan rushing around to get me ready and onto the school bus. With my bag packed ready for what today brought I made it to school on time. I walked through the gate with my head hung low shuffling my way through the entrance hoping no-one saw me, but without any hesitation Grace came running up to me.

"Hey Lou, I've missed you" she begins "I'm sorry I've ignored you I felt sorry for Tracey, so I made friends with her"

Uncertain whether Grace was telling the truth or whether this was a trick I just look down to her without saying a word.

"Are we still friends?" Grace asks almost begging me.

"Sure" I replied without any emotion.

To be honest I felt uneasy and just wanted Grace to walk off but instead she picked bag up and rummaging through it then gave me a big pat on the back before running into the playground. I walked up the path towards the playground. There were children running past me laughing pointing directly at me. What's going on I thought.

"Stay away" one shouted laughing at me. Literally everyone was running past me laughing or staying apart I just didn't understand. It was only when I reached the playground when Mrs Vape ripped a piece of paperwork off my back which had the words 'be warned I have wind'.

"Who's done this?" Mrs Vape shouts.

I looked around the playground to see Grace and Tracey giggling to themselves. Guilty as charged I thought to myself. So there goes making friends with these two. The whole playground was full of laughter-at my expense. Saved by the morning bell. We all lined up ready to go in.

Break time soon came around. I dreaded this time; it was the only time I truly felt alone with no friends. I had to find somewhere to go where no one else was, to save anyone saying anything or laughing at me. Thankfully, things get forgotten in schools quickly, by the time break time came along those that knew what had happened had moved on to something else. I walked the perimeter of the playground with nowhere to hide I found myself on the field once again. Slumped up the tree, I finally lost it and started to cry. I no longer felt I could cope with this school and how I felt being here. I put my head into my hands and let out the tears. Then all of sudden I felt something, something in my belly that told me I was going to be ok. I suddenly felt ok like I didn't have anything to worry about. I just didn't understand. I slowly lifted my head up to see the young girl was here again, but this time she stood in front of me. Still with her back to me but she was in reaching distance. I didn't know whether to approach her, but she was stood right in my way, so I had to acknowledge her.

"Excuse me" I said politely

Yet again I had no response, losing my patience with this girl I began to shout

"Right, I've had it trying with you"

I stormed off to my right to be stood right in front of her. She was wearing the same boots as yesterday and clothes from the 1800's she had just got out the bin, they were ripped and dirty. Her long black hair was covering her face. I reached forward to move her hair away from her face to discover, she wasn't normal looking. I stood still for a moment my mouth wide open gobsmacked at what I could see. "What on earth" I said under my breath.

She didn't look anything like us. To start with she only had one eye, her eye was in the middle of her forehead, big and black in colour and extremely blood shot, her nose spread across her face and her lips seemed to be glued and then stappled shut. She lifted her head, moving her one eye towards the top to look at me. At this point I didn't know what to do. I began to become anxious, my heart beating fast with all sorts rushing around my head.

"Don't hurt me" I pleaded I'll give you anything" I continued.

She just stared at me. No movement. The more I looked at her the wider her eye became. She reached out her hand, she had very long fingers, but half of her hand was purple and really veiny, I certainly wasn't taking it. She clicked her neck to the left and suddenly she started to grow taller, I looked down to realise she was actually hovering above me about a foot off the ground. I fell to the ground, with my heart racing. I used all the strength within me to push myself backwards away from the girl. The more I moved the quicker I was swept towards her. It was as if she was flying within a milli second, we were face to face. I shut my eyes and screamed as loud as I could. Until I heard that familiar voice again.

"What's wrong Louise?" Shouted Mrs Vape running towards me.

I opened my eyes to see Mrs Vape standing in front of me, the whole of the fence was filled with the children laughing at me. I was breathing that fast, I started to hyperventilate, I had spots in my eyes. I was shaking violently.

"It was her- where was she?" I asked looking around.

"Where was what? You threw yourself on the floor and started screaming, you were alone" Mrs Vape replied worried.

"You don't understand, there was a girl, a girl with only one eye and a nose the same size as her face" I began to explain "She was hovering in the air"

Helping me off the floor Mrs Vape was overly concerned in what I was saying.

"Honestly, Louise there was no one on the field with you, you were the only one"

I was taken straight to the headmaster's office. On my walk down to the office I realised how crazy I sounded. I sat there uncertain what was going to happen. The headmaster, Mr Gerald appeared wearing his favourite grey suit he always wore. After asking me serval questions on what had happened, he brought the school therapist in. I was still adamant there was something on the field with me they decided to watch the video back. To them I looked like I was having a fit. Through the eyes of everyone else watching that video I was crying in my hands one minute, then jumped up walked around in a circle and then threw myself on the floor shaking, but to me I didn't see the same, I saw the girl I was looking at on the field. It had happened again. Something I couldn't explain.

CHAPTER 4

Things start to get weird

After time I just got used to the fact, I could see things no one else could, and see things that were going to happen before they happened. I just thought I had special abilities; they just became my normal life. It was only when I started high school things got a-bit out of my control. Everywhere I turned I never knew who was real or who was in fact inside my head, do I talk to them or not. I didn't want my first couple of months in high school to start off on the wrong foot and become the weird child no one wanted to talk to again! The child who talks to herself. So, I started off as a-bit of a loner to be honest, while I worked out who I could trust and who I couldn't. Until I met Darcey. Darcey was in my class and just like me she was reserved; she would just sit in the corner of the room. We would often look at each other as if to say I know how you feel, but did we truly know how each other felt? A couple of months into the school year we were given a science project which had to be done in pairs, Grace was no longer in my class, so I didn't have that horrible sinking feeling of not being picked by your so-called best friend, we were however still friends in case you were wondering. We would often meet up at lunch time to see how our day was going but that was about it. So, wondering what was going to happen and deciding who was paired up with who, the teacher had the bright idea of letting us choose our own partners. The rush of embarrassment appeared over me once again, why do we have to do projects in pairs I thought to myself, I'm quite happy being alone. I thought I would just wait on my chair to see who was left when everyone had finished picking, but to my happiness and excitement I looked round before everyone had even started walking around to Darcey stood right in front me.

"Would you like to be my partner" she asked politely in a soft and gentle voice. Without any hesitation I turned round and spoke

"Of course,"

but then a confusion on how she even got in front of me.

"Hang on – how did u even get over here, no one had even moved?" I asked.

Darcey just looked at me with a slight grin.

We started the science project, I either went to Darcey's or she came to mine. Darcey only lived down the road from me, her mom and dad worked all hours just like mine, only she didn't have a nanny so we could do what we wanted at hers. The first couple of days we did actually do the project, but we started to get more comfortable with each other as time went by and by the end of the week, we did more talking then working. I finally felt like a proper kid, I was doing things everyone my age was doing. We spent a lot of time together- Darcey became my best friend. The more time we spent together the more I realised we were more similar then first anticipated. We dressed the same, we had the same personalities and the same frame build. Things were finally looking up for me. These great days only lasted for a while before the usual feelings and sights I saw started getting worse. Literally everywhere I turned I was seeing these people, the old cowboy or cowgirl type, the ones no-one else could see. I didn't want to draw attention to this, I had a good friendship with Darcey I didn't want to scare her away. They just happened to appear right in front of me now, before they kept their distance but now, they walked straight through me. The first time it happened it was a strange sensation. I could actually feel their souls rip through mine. It startled me. I started walking a couple of meters away from Darcey, so she didn't notice anything. The strange thing was the more time I spent with her the more of these cowboys I would see.

We agreed on this particular Friday we would get a take-away- we opted for pizza to share. We picked a film, while her mom and dad were out working, I didn't ask her at the time what her parents did, but they were never in much. They must have worked hard I thought. So, it was just the two of us. To get some fresh air we decided to fetch the pizza ourselves it was only at the top of the road. It was my first ever sleep over, so I was usually tucked up in the house after dark, this was a rare occasion to be walking around. We picked what we wanted and set out, walking up the road I noticed that there were more than then the usual cowboys out at night. Trying not to take notice I struggled to think of a conversation topic to start. We almost reached the pizza shop before I had even started.

"Wow, that didn't take us long" I said quickly trying to say something-anything. Darcey looked at me with a smile. Darcey was easy going and was quite happy with silence when we were together. I looked back up to notice that there was one right in front of Darcey.

Oops I thought to myself, what's going to happen here is she is going to walk straight through him? I can't warn her obviously she will think I'm crazy, while I was debating how to distract her to my amazement the cowboy flipped his hat and she saluted him. Did she actually just do that or am I seeing things? I wasn't sure whether to react or just ignore what I had just seen. Scared of losing the only friend I had, I decided to just pick the pizza up as if nothing had happened. We made it back to Darcey's still not saying anything it was chewing me up from the inside. Could Darcey not feel the tension in the room? I couldn't concentrate on the film we were watching at all, I needed to know if she actually saw him. I slowly turned to face Darcey who was sat on the chair to the left of me ready to confront the elephant in the room, unknown to me she was actually asleep, curled up in a ball. Well I guess it will have to wait for now I said to myself. I turned the tv off and snuggled up on the other chair with the throw that was available. I tossed and turned for a while, over thinking everything that had happened that day. I finally feel asleep when I was suddenly woken by a loud bang. Keeping my eyes closed, anxious of what I might see I lay there, waiting to hear what I thought may have been Darcey's Mom and Dad. But no other sound continued. Confused I slowly opened my eyes to check everything was ok-Darcey wasn't on the chair. Feeling uneasy on my first sleepover I wanted to look where she was. I searched the kitchen in case she had gone for a drink-the kitchen was clear. Maybe she had got uncomfortable on the chair and decided to go to her room but that too was clear. I knew she hadn't gone in her parents' room that was forbidden. I began to get nervous, surely, she wouldn't have left me in her house on my own. I made my way back downstairs and noticed the garage light was shining through the small gap under the old wooden double door.

Trying not to be too loud to wake the neighbours I shouted "Darcey, what are you doing out here?"
"Darcey" I repeated getting closer, but there was no response. I tried to open the garage door, but it was locked, trying again and again I had no joy.
"Darcey, are you in there? I don't really like being out here on my own" I shouted through the keyhole. I still had no answer. I just wanted to go home.
 I noticed there was a window around the other side of the garage. I slowly made my way around. The garden was pitch black other than the reflection of the garage light, every other step I took I cracked a tree branch that was on the floor, trying not to wake any neighbours I slowed my pace down. The fence to my right started to rattle, I quickly looked up to see two big green eyes staring at me. I stood as still as a statue I didn't know whether to run inside or scream. I looked for a couple of seconds, then the green eyes suddenly blinked and let out a meow, I realised it was next doors cat. I continued my journey round to the window.
"Please Darcey be in here" I whispered to myself. I tiptoed to look through the glass- she wasn't in there either. The garage was full of old bits and bobs, old car parts, boxes and bags which looked to be filled with all sorts of stuff, old cameras. Maybe it was all the stuff they didn't want in the house but couldn't part with. Either way it was no business of mine. Just as I went to turn round, there was a picture

hung on the wall. This picture was scenic, it was a long pathway with serval trees going up the paths, either side had a grass verge on and a couple of benches on. The more I looked at the picture the more I thought the trees were moving, as if the wind were blowing them.

"Surely not" I said. I squinted my eyes with a quick shake of my head I moved my eyes away from the picture onto the floor of the garage. I couldn't believe what I was seeing – sat there on a slight slant in a A4 sized black frame was a picture. A picture of the extract cowboy I had seen at the theme park many years ago.

"What, how do they know him?" I panicked

I shot back almost falling to the floor, trying to catch my breath I saw a big white light coming out of the garage. I quickly stood up holding onto the window ledge just my legs dangling. I looked through the window to see the picture on the wall shaking from side to side, casually walking down the path was something walking towards me. The light got brighter and brighter and began to spin, getting faster and faster, when suddenly falling out of the painting on her hands and knees was Darcey.

CHAPTER 5

Where I truly belong

I couldn't believe what I had just seen, I stood in total shock. Staring at Darcey on the floor-she clearly didn't know I was there. I didn't know whether to make her aware I was there or quickly try to hide before she catches me, but it was too late. Darcey started to walk towards the garage door. I could feel myself start to panic, frantically looking either side of me for something to hide behind. Before I knew it, the garage door swung open. Darcey brushing herself down like she had just tripped and fallen over. She turned to her left to find me stood there staring at her. "Lou, you gave me a fright, what are you doing out here? Been here long?" she whispered.

I gave you a fright I thought to myself.

"I heard a noise in your house, and I couldn't find you, I noticed the light on in the garage so I come to find you, but you weren't in there a minute ago and then... Well," I answered back.

But before I could finish my sentence, Darcey replied, "I think me, and you need to have a chat, come on back in its cold out here"

We slowly made our way back into her house. How could she be so normal I thought to myself, how is it even possible for her to just do what she has done and then to act the way she is, not even an explanation or anything. Surly she knows I've seen everything. Or does she not? I started to doubt if she even knows, shill I just ignore I seen anything, deny it when she asks me?

All this was going through my head while we were walking down her garden.

We made it back into her kitchen.

"Do you want a drink?" she asked me.

"Sure, why not, a cold one if I can please" I replied

She made us our drinks and we went and sat on the sofa. I could feel the tension in the room. Which one of us is going to cut it first.

"So, what Is it we need to talk about" I said quickly, not handling the suspense any longer.

Darcey took a long sip of her coke and turned to face me.

"Do you not find it weird how we became such best friends, when you couldn't settle in with anyone-you were always on your own, different to everyone else? So why do me and you get along so well?" Darcey starting the conversation.

"Well, I just thought. hang on how do u know I've always been alone" I asked sharply.

"Lou- I've known you since you were born, I know everything about you." Darcey replied.

I sat there frozen in my chair, staring at Darcey but not actually looking at her. How can she know everything about me? I thought to myself.

"Look Darcey this is creeping me out, we haven't been friends long and I know what I've just seen in the garage anyone else wouldn't be sat here right now if they had seen the same as me" I said puzzled.

"That's the thing Lou- Me and you aren't normal, we are far from it, Me and you are the same, this is why I've been sent to be your friend, to show you the way. I know we see the same things; I know everything that you have seen. I didn't plan on telling you this quick or even in this way but now is the time you have seen too much for me to tell you, but We are both" A long silence came from Darcey before she eventually slowly looked up at me, my face more puzzled then ever she whispered

"We're Immortal!"

"Immortal" I shouted.

"Yes, and that's not all we have special powers" She smiles

"Immortal-With special powers, no this is wrong you must have the wrong person" I shouted shaking my head, sweating, and rocking from side to side.

"No defiantly not, you remember the cowboy at the theme park?" she asked

Nodding my head in disbelief she even knew that had happened to me.

"That's my dad- your dad best friend" she replied

"No- I would have seen him around the house before now surly-my dad always has his work friends around" I answered sure I knew the answer.

"Opps sorry Lou, I forgot to mention your Mum and Dad that you know aren't your real parents- you surely didn't think a bloodmoth could of gave birth to you, do you?"

"Wait what is a bloodmoth and what do you mean they

aren't my parents"

All I wanted to do was wake up, surly all this needed to be a dream. Wake up Wake Up I shouted to myself, hitting my head trying to get my own attention.

"Lou, this isn't a dream" I could slightly hear over my own thoughts.

I opened my eyes to realise this wasn't a dream I was still sat in Darcey's.

"I know this is a lot to take in and I know you must have a lot of question, but please ask me. Don't just sit there confused." Darcey said concerned.

I sat there for a moment or two going over and over in my head. There were so many questions I had, where do I start? Gathering my thoughts together I began.

"Ok One- What is a BloodMoth, Two-How are my parents not my parents, do they know I'm not theirs?" I said frantically

Darcey turned to smile at me.

"Wow one a time" she replies.

"A Bloodmoth is a 'normal' human being- not immortal, Your Parents – your real parents are amazing, Marley and Leon, they are 300 years old, and a big part of our world" Darcey said so normal.

I just couldn't believe what I was hearing. Have you ever heard something you know just couldn't be true? This was one of those moments. I knew she was going to turn round and say, 'I got you good then didn't I'. but that never happened it was all true!

"Our parents started our world off, my parents are 400 years old, they eventually came across your parents." She finished.

"Marley and Leon made the heartbroken decision to give you up at birth, in hope for you to have a normal life, when you were born, our world was having a lot of problems. There's a family 'the Cloudy's', who wants to destroy all of us hoping to overtake and your parents didn't want to put you in that kind of danger, so they sent me to guide you through. They have been watching you and miss you terribly, they found Shelly and David, they watched them for months and because they worked a lot, they knew they wouldn't click onto your difference and it worked, they don't have a clue, do they? "Darcey began to explain. "Now I know you've taken in a lot of information but is there anything else you want to ask me?" she questioned.

"What about the painting, I saw you coming back through it "I replied.

Darcey smiled "Do you want to see?"

Before I could even speak, I found myself in the garage feeling sick, the room was spinning.

"What's just happened?" I shouted.

"You will get used it-it speed change" Darcey explained. "it's where you can change your destination in a second to anywhere in the world"

"There's a lot I've got to learn by the looks of it" I replied rubbing my belly, hiccupping, wondering how long this sick feeling was going to last.

I slowly made my way up still unsteady on my feet.

"Don't rush up to fast, you will just fall straight back down" Darcey Smiled.

I decided to sit back on the floor, looking around me-looking how normal this garage looked after all the whole family looked normal to me, I thought I was the odd one out here. Darcey started walking over to the painting, I watched in disbelief. As soon as she got to the painting, a man appeared from nowhere. creeping around the trees, he was the size of my fingernail.

"it's ok albert, she's with me-she's the daughter of the big Lord! You can come out" Darcey began to say.

"The Big Lord? what on earth is happening here" I whispered to myself. Still staring not, a clue what is going on. I'm in two minds weather to get closer or just run for my life.

"Come here-Lou" Darcey said quietly.

She reached her hand out to help me up, still slightly unstable I stand to my feet.

"Albert- this is Lou- the daughter of Marley and Leon"

"The Marley and Leon" chocked Albert.

My real parents must be really important I thought to myself, how is it possible me Lou from up the road, the one people just walk past, the invisible one. This is crazy!

"Come closer dear" the man from the painting shouted directly at me.

Without thinking I made my way to the painting, unsure whether to speak or just stand there but before I could even open my mouth, he begins

"Your, Your Mothers double" he says fascinated looking at me from head to toe.

Not knowing exactly how to answer him I just looked at Darcey for any reassurance. I didn't know whether to be scared. I felt like I didn't have any emotion right now I was numb to everything going on around me. Darcey was smiling like she finally had a weight lifted off her. Albert staring at me through the picture, there was an awkward silence.

"Well, I know a lot of people who are waiting to meet you- are you coming in?" Albert asked impatiently.

"I don't know how to do it" I replied concerned.

"I'll show you" Laughed Darcey.

"All you need to do is run towards the painting and say your dads name three times, as soon as you say it the last time the portal will open, and you can jump straight in-watch me" Darcey finished.

She took three large steps back and started running towards the picture "Amado, Amado, Amado"
"Wait I've forgotten my dad's name" I shouted just before she got to the painting. On her way through Darcey shouts "It will come to you as you get closer" her voice fading as she disappeared.

Great! I thought to myself, how am I supposed to do this now, Darcey has disappeared and so has Albert. Debating whether to just throw in the towel and go home or go through and find my true meaning and where I'm from- I mean what would you do if you were a nobody like me? What time is it? Are Shelly and David wondering where I am, it's getting light out there do you think it's time for me to go? All these things running through my head at the same time as trying to remember what my 'real' Dads name was. I began to walk up and down the garage pacing the area. Biting my nails when Albert appeared back whispering "Leon, your dads name- come on in" Before he sharply disappeared gain.

I felt like I didn't have a choice, like they were all waiting for me. Walking up to the painting to have a closer look I reached out, hoping my hand would just go straight through it, but that never happened. It felt like a normal painting. Rough parts where the paint hadn't dried properly before someone had touched it. If my hand wouldn't go through, then how is my whole body supposed to I began to worry.

"Well, I guess there's no answer to my question although then to go for it so here goes nothing." I convinced myself.

I took the slowest steps back I possibly could, finally reaching the end of the garage, I took a deep breath in and out.

"What if the portal doesn't open" the last thought that ran through my head. I lifted my left leg ready to start my run, my heartbeat throbbing in my throat.

"Leon, Leon Leon" I shouted running towards a big brick garage wall, with just a picture hanging in the middle. I have everything riding on this portal opening or I'm going to be very bruised if not. As I got closer to the painting the brightest light appeared in a star shape getting bigger and bigger, it felt like it took me ages, the next thing I was spinning in circles which looked like straight through a black hole, then all of a sudden hundreds of memories started to appear around me as if I was reliving everything that had happened to me but from the outside looking in. The loudest screaming you could possibly hear, then it fell eery silent. I was floating in mid-air; I could see the greenest of grass underneath me as if it weren't real, and without warning I fell face first into the grass. I lay still for a moment or two before I realised, I had made it- I was finally through the painting.

CHAPTER 6

The other side

I have one word for this place 'Amazing' it was nothing that I expected I thought it was going to be bare, dark, and gloomy. But it was the complete opposite, the sun was blaring, there were flowers everywhere-every colour you could think of, big ones, small ones. The colour of everything here was more vibrant than anywhere before, it was like nothing was actually real- I mean was things real here I had no idea. I turned over to sit on my bum, looking around side to side there was just grass and flowers every-where. I turned around to look behind me and in the far distance it looked like a forest, there must have been over 300 trees. Wondering where Darcey was, I thought she may have met me here -after all I didn't even know where to go. I decided to make my way towards the forest, everything was so calm here you couldn't even feel scared if you try to.

You feel free!

As I got closer to the forest, it was so pretty I never knew how picturise one place could be I loved it here already! The huge trees hung over the light brown path inter twining with each other they made a canopy over the top. There were skinny ones, fat ones. Bushy one all sorts. I started walking down the path running in and out of the trees, looking up at sky the smile on my face was like no other before. This place makes you feel so different, a feeling I've never had. I felt as if I could do anything in this world- as if it were possible for me Lou to be able to do that. Although I felt like nothing in this world could change my amazing news, I knew I was here for a reason. To find out who I truly was and meet my real parents. I started to panic. What if they don't like me, what if I'm to normal for them? All these things started running through my head. The calm and free feeling I had has suddenly disappeared. I found myself reaching the end of the path confused on where I should go next. I started to feel like I wanted to get out of here, this needed to end. The more I thought about it the more I realised I couldn't even get out if I wanted to, where was the exit? My breathing started to get faster. I knew I was entering a state of panic. There was no one around, I found my self alone once again in my life!

As I reached the end of the path it was a cross rounds. Left or right I thought to myself. What do I have to lose either way I don't know where I'm going to end up? Both sides looked identical. My first thought was telling me right, but my heart was telling me left. My heart has never given me the right choice before so why should I listen to it now I thought. I began to start turning right, my right foot first quickly followed by my left when all of a sudden, this big grey cloud appeared in front of me. Inside this cloud was a man, a man I have never seen before. He had long white hair, with a long whitist grey beard, the palest of blue eyes. He let out the biggest smile ever. I shot back onto floor. Shocked.

"Turn around" he said in a croaky voice. "This is the wrong way" he continued.

"Who are you?" I answered

"It doesn't matter, just listen to me now!" he said abruptly. Within a second, he was vanished.

Now even more interested, all I wanted to do was take this path. Do I listen to a man I've never met before or go with my gut instinct? I've never been told what to do before I make my own choice. So without a second thought I started to walk down the right hand side of the path, I started to walk slowly, half of me is wondering have I choose right and the other half of me is weirdly hoping the man in the cloud will appear to tell me again. I reached halfway down when I suddenly decided I needed to turn back. I had a funny feeling about this. I turned around. The path seemed to look a lot longer. Is it just my eyes or has it grown? As I started to make my way back up the path it was as if it was closing in on me. I started to run faster and faster trying all I could to make it back, but it was too late, I reached the end. The path had closed off. The end of path had a brick wall there was no-way back through. I placed both my hands on the wall hoping that someway it would disappear, and I could make it through. I bowed my head, finally realising I should of listen. I looked back up to see the cloud appearing again. He shook his head and began

"You should have listened girl. Now you must face the con-sequences. I can't promise it won't be unpleasant"

I took a deep swallow. Well, what do I do now, there is only one way out? I turned to face the long path, which now has changed its appearance it no longer has that calm and relaxing feeling, neither was it bright and colourful. It was like I was somewhere different. I suddenly had all my fear and anxiousness back. I froze for a minute. I know I need to start moving but my legs have turned to jelly. I can't stay here. I picked up the courage and made my way down. The trees started to blow violently as I walked past them, spinning in circles, and swiping down inches away from hitting me to the floor. I could feel something was wrong here, but what choice do I have now. I started to run hoping I could make it to the other end quicker. In the distance I could see a shadow, I can't make out what exactly it is, as I got closer, I could see it was hairy. I stayed two meters back just to be sure what it was. This shadow started emerging from behind the tree, it was a tall figure, wearing a long cloak, his face, neck, and hands were covered in thick black hair. His eyes were a deep red. I wasn't sure whether to be scared or just ignore the fact I could see him- am I seeing things no one else can as usual?

"Look at you" the figure started.

"Well how did you find yourself down here, it's not a place for a girl like you. With that being said there's only one way out now girl and that's through this door" he finished.

Behind the figure sat a large brown wooden door, with a round black metal handle in the middle. The door didn't look uninviting, just like any other door. Without thinking I stepped closer just about to reach out to touch the handle. When the figure shouted.

"Don't! I've not told you the rules"

Eager to just get out of here I didn't think.

"Rules, what rules I'm just trying to get to my parents, they will know how I can get back" I said quickly trying to rush him on.

"Your parents hey, and who may they be" he said rubbing his thick hair on his face.

Staring at the ground trying to quickly remember their names.

"Erm Leon and Marley" I replied shocked I remembered.

Before I knew it, the figure was basically touching my nose, he had swooped down without even moving, he was eye to eye to me, swooping in circler motions he says

"Hmm the daughter of the one and only Marley and Leon I see, well I expect great things form you"

I tried to catch him turning around each time he did but he didn't have any legs he was quicker than me. He only had a torso, arms, and head.

"Well, what are the rules" I questioned.

"You do have a brave heart, the rules are simple girl, you make it out the other end without cheating and your through" he smiled.

"It's that simple!" I laughed.

"Don't be fooled girl-you'll see what I mean" he said quickly while spinning in circles disappearing.

I stood there silently, just looking around. I know I can do this; how hard can it be I just make it through. Just as I went to step forward the grey cloud appears again, the man with the grey beard and pale blue eyes staring at me.

"Knock your confidence down, you'll never make it out, oh and one more thing never give eye contact to the three eyed slimeball" he whispers.

"Three eyed slimeball" I replied confused, but within a second, he was gone.

Maybe this isn't as easy as it looks, I thought to myself. Maybe I need to rethink this, isn't there another way out I questioned. Clearly not.

"Well here goes nothing" I said to myself. I slowly made my way towards the door, I reached out to touch the handle, but as I got closer, I could feel heat, this intense heat. I turned the handle and without warning these great big balls of fire came spinning towards me. I quickly slammed the door shut leaning my back on it, praying, and hoping this fire ball would just collapse on the floor, it was inches from my face when it let out a loud scream and crumbled to the floor. Breathing heavily, I dropped to my knees in total shock I wasn't burnt to a crisp. I brushed myself off and stood there looking.

"Oh no a maze" I said ", I couldn't pick the right path the first time I'm bound to pick the wrong one now.

Right in front of me was a room.

"Hi, I'm Taz the fluff bunny" shouted this round floating blue thing, stood in front of me. I jumped back thinking how many more of these things are around here.

"Don't worry, I'm here to help you, not hurt you, this way" he shouted.

I can't believe I've just started following this blue fluffy bunny, what have I become- I was desperate to get out. Taz had long white vampire fangs and his teeth rotated as he spoke. He looked cute but also scary at the same time, but he seemed to want to help me and he's the best option I have right now.

Taz spoke softly as if he was young, he acted like a child too, wanting to play.

"Taz, where are you taking me" I asked quickly.

"Don't worry, I will show you the way, but its not easy, you have to use all the courage and bravery you have" Taz started to explain.

"If you make it out then your free, if you don't then you will be stuck here, like me" he continued.

"How long have you been here?" I asked politely.

"I've been here 250 years, I took the same route as you, but I didn't make it out the other side, so I've been trapped here ever since" he cried.

"I've seen hundreds of people make it through I know the right way and the wrong way so stick with me and I'll show you the way." He Finished.

He ran off spinning in the air shouting "Wahoo, we have a new contestant, roll up roll up guys here she goes"

"All you have to do is follow the track and complete each puzzle to get to the next level, sounds simple but there's a hidden twist in every level" Taz explained.

"Do you have any question before you start, because once you do puzzle one, I can no longer help you" Taz finished.

"No, I guess I'll just start". I replied anxious.

CHAPTER 7

Will I make it

I made my way towards puzzle one, unsure what I was going to come across, swissing in the coroner of the room was a little Nome minding his own business-fiddling with something on the wall, whistling to himself.

"Excuse me" while clearing my throat.

"Oh, dear you gave me a freight, no one has been through this door in a very long time." The Nome replied.

As he turned around, he was wearing a pointed red hat, his pointy ears stuck out the sides. He was about 3-foot-high, wearing a red jacket with black trousers and red squared boots.

"Listen here girl, you have three levels, this one is simple, the next one is medium and the last well let's put it this way you finish the last level then you're a true Gorgon"

"Gorgon" I questioned through a frown.

"Yes" he replied I could see he was wondering why I was there if I didn't even understand the simplest of things in 'their' world.

"A Gorgon- is an immortal person" he explained

"So, let me get this straight a bloodmoth is a non-immortal and we are Gorgon's" I said curiously

"you're learning girl" he smiled. "Now what are you doing here, I gathered you had taken the wrong path, but what brings you to this beautiful island of Gubble Gom"

Gubble Gom? Another new word I thought to myself.

"I'm trying to find my parents; you may know them?" I began

"Marley and Le..." But before I could even finish, he interrupted me.

"The Marley and Leon? Come on now girl you best get cracking there be waiting" he said abruptly while shoving me towards this big square in the middle of the room. This square was lite up green round the edges and the inside was shiny red.

"Now watch closely a bird will appear and you must copy the same pattern he does, you do it correctly and he will drop the key for the door, understand? "He explains.

"Sure, got it" I smiled.

This seemed too easy I thought. Then within a second this huge yellow bird emerged; his wings were so big I almost fell backwards with the power off them. He hovered in mid-air flapping his wings glaring at me with his huge green eyes. He lent towards me opened his mouth and threw out a huge ball of fire. I tilted my head to the right to try and avoid the flame burning me. He turned his back on me and started to move around. Left right up down and back to the middle.

'It's the letter L" I shouted to myself. I do the letter L and land back in the middle,

"simple"

Chuffed with myself I moved towards the first square. Just as I stood on the first square, the room went pitch black. I could feel the square starting to rock back and forth underneath me, then the sound of wings, little, tiny wings surround both ears, I could feel something all over my body. The lights came back on. To my horror there were tiny little bugs flying all around me. These tiny bugs had clear wings with a grey body. I frantically started to wave both arms to try and escape them. I looked for my next square to the right of me, I can see it. It was in reaching distance, I gave a big swoop of my arms and jumped to the next square. It fell eerily quiet. I stood for a moment expecting the worse, but nothing happened I quickly looked for my next square. Jumping in front of me I made it, without a second thought I jumped to my next one.

"One more left" I quietly said to myself.

I stood for a moment, wondering what was next. Just as I stood on the last square, the huge bird appeared, flapping his wings once again, looking at me furiously. He hovered in mid-air his wings spread out to steady him, he threw out a huge flame of fire and started flying around me. I could feel my palms starting to sweat, my heart beating so fast I could feel it pumping through my t-shirt. I froze. Thinking to myself what do I do here, do I just let him do his thing around me? Will he just disappear again? I was so confused. The room started spinning, everything seemed to be getting on top of me.

"I don't know what you want me to do" I screamed out crying. Suddenly I found myself airborne, the same height as the bird, I throw my arms out in front of me, this lightning bolt came gushing out the tips of my fingers. It hit the bird and he let out a cry, spinning almost touching the floor. He span his head around, looking even more angry he shot back in the air, he gave his wings a shake and this long silver spike appeared on each one, he did a Criss cross motion of his wings and started marching towards me, quick thinking I ducked. Narrowly missing him I catch my breath. Having no idea how I managed to do the lightning bolt, I felt stuck, and my life was about to be over. I closed my eyes, hoping and praying something would happen, and just like that I found myself shooting at the bird once again. I hit him straight in the chest and he span in circles, tucking his wings underneath him, almost a ball shape. He drops to fall. Panting I look around me, half expecting something else to happen. I froze once again. I turned to face the middle square. This huge bright white light started emerging from the middle, I covered my eyes with my arm, feeling the light still piercing my eyes. It went dark. I slowly emerged to find a shiny key just floating halfway up. I ran as quick as I could, opened the next door and collapsed. I was now in level 2.

Not over the bird yet I sat on the floor holding my head in between my legs, to frightened to even want to know what was next in stall for me. If level 1 was meant to be easy then I have no chance, I thought. Nevertheless, it is now or never. I looked up; it was quiet. No-one around, there was no Taz, no Nome-nothing. Do I just begin I wondered? Right in front of me was a tall green entrance, running all the way down was green bushes, they must have been 8 feet tall, that was all I could see. The entrance must have been the size of foot path, it looked like it got narrower as it reached the end. I must run straight to the end as quick as I can I presumed. I put my right foot across to start, and you guessed it the atmosphere changed, a huge black cloud lingered over me, as if I had turned a switch on. Here we go I guessed, almost used of something happening. Looking around me I felt eager for whatever it was would just appear so I could start. The black cloud started spinning above me opening in the centre, four huge figures dropped down. They all had square heads, almost as if they didn't have any skin, they looked transparent. Their eyes were bright green in the shape of a diamond. They were wearing a black top which looked like they had shoulder pads on, with three silver spikes on top, their legs were an inch thick and transparent. As they landed to the floor, they dropped with one leg bent in front of them landing on their left hand, they slowly lifted their head to daze at me. I shot back, terrified. Unsure of their next move, I froze just looking at them. It was like a stare off I wasn't sure if they were waiting for me to make the first move or them. They looked at each other and suddenly fire started to come out their backs, I knew we had started. They surrounded me in a circle two at the back of me and two in front of me, they hovered looking down at me. Giggling away to each other. I again found myself panicking, I tried to calm myself down taking deep breaths in and out. My body shaking, I have no alternative but to do something. I started to run but through my panic state, I stumbled all over the place, dropping to the floor. I pushed myself back up looking behind me to see if they were still there. They were following me. As I ran forwarded, I found myself in the middle of a maze, which is the right way I wondered. My gut told me to turn left, so that is what I did. I looked in front of me hoping I could see the exit, but then I come to realise the maze was moving, in and out, left to right. I was running for my life. I looked back and realised I had made it halfway through, not so bad I thought to myself. Then everything changed, right in front of me a ball of fire landed spreading a couple of inches either side. I turned round in horror, to see the figures throwing fire balls at me through the spikes in their shoulder pads. They all throw two fireballs each, I was jumping to dodge them running in and out of the stretch fire burning on the floor. I felt this hot rush twingling between my toes reaching the top of my legs, without any warning I was airborne facing the figures without any control I was throwing lightning bolts at them. I landed back on the ground to find myself running faster, the faster I got the faster they became until they were right behind me. I span around and threw a lightning bolt at the closest one to me, they span round and crumpled to the floor.

"Wohho" got one I shouted fist pumping the air.

Still running I had managed to shoot down two more. Only the one left.

In a machinable voice the last one shouts "you must kill me to escape, I'm Xrex, the king of all Rex's"

"Rex's" I shouted back.

"You really don't know this world do you" he replied shooting me with his fire balls.

"Rex's are a dangerous creature who live here at gooble gom, you will not make it out of here" he continued running faster to me when he stopped inches from my face. He let out a loud

"Roar!"

The next thing I know he shot six fire balls at me, I tried to dodge all six, but every way I turned the fire balls chased me. I tried to outrun them but one stubborn one remand, the next thing I was hit. I stumbled rolling on the floor when I suddenly hit the grass hedge face down. The pain rushed through my whole body. I felt paralysed. I lay still for what seemed forever when I finally lifted my head. Xrex was staring at me hoping I was dead.

"Tough cookie" he shouted directly at me.

This anger started to manifest itself all over, I could feel my head was about to explode. I stood with pride, lifted my arms and out of nowhere, all 10 fingertips started to pulse, and they let out a web of lighting. Catching Xrex and twinning all around him, I pulled him towards me. The strength I had was unreal. Now having Xrex in my hands I lifted him in the air before finally letting him drop. I released my web as he started to fall, I shot 10 lightning bolts straight at him. He violently shook on the floor rolling and rolling before finally coming to a stop. He started to disintegrate into the ground as he disappeared, he left the shinny key on the floor. Picking the key up I had made another level.

I casually made my way towards the next door, still shocked and in disbelief over the last two levels, I had learnt so much about myself already. I knew I could run extremely fast, I had unbelievable strength and my fingertips had lightning bolts in them. Feeling invisible I made my way to level 3. I opened the door, to find just a field. Level 3 had a different feeling. I didn't feel scared. I calmly walked towards the centre of the field. The out shirks were surrounded in trees. Like a forest was the other end. I could see the exit door in the far-left hand side. Do I make my way over I wondered? I didn't want to make any sudden movements so not changing my pace I started to walk towards the door. As I got closer, the trees in front of me started to slightly move side to side, before getting faster in a swissing motion, getting faster and faster. My heart started to pick up a bigger and faster beat. The tree suddenly parted down the middle, in the distance I could see something kicking its back leg, sliding it back and forth ready to pounce. This thing started belting towards me. As it got closer, I notice something, three eyes glaring at me, three huge red circled eyes. I shot back onto the floor just my hands to stop me from collapsing fully to the ground.

"The three eyed slimeball, don't give it eye contact" I kept mumbling to myself trying to look anywhere but at him. It was still running towards me.

"You made it" it shouted to me through his huge, pointed teeth.

The outer shell of the slimeball was black with red spikes all over it, he had four legs hanging out his huge round body, they were also covered in red spikes. He came right up to me; I couldn't help but look at him. His huge red eyes started getting enormous, this unbearable pain shocking through my whole body. I dropped to my knees covering my ears, dropping my head down.

"Do not look me in the eye girl" he roared at me.

"You could of escaped here with no harm, if you had paid attention in the first place, there is no puzzle here, no dwell with Xrex, you escape with great courage and unselfishness" he explain in his massive deep roar of a voice.

"I don't understand" I said confused.

"It's simple girl, you make a choice, I take you, or I take them" pointing behind me.

I turned around, and stood behind me, were two people. The man looked identical to the man that was in the grey cloud the same grey beard and grey hair. He was wearing a long white cloak he stood with his feet slightly apart smiling at me. Stood next to the man was a woman, she had glorious blonde curly hair, pale blue eyes. She was wearing a long white dress with white sandals. She turned to look at me with this beautiful smile. I stood looking at them wondering what to do now. neither of them said a word, the man just put his arm out and pointed to the slimeball.

"So, it's that simple, you or them" he asked.

I looked around me, turning from the two people back to the slimeball, making sure I didn't look him in the eye. Without thinking I instantly said

"Me, take me" I screamed dropping to the floor.

I didn't know what was next. The field fell silent. I sat on the floor, heartbroken. I didn't know if I was going to be alive in the next 5 minutes. Was he going to kill me, or keep me here? My mind was in overdrive. I decided to pluck the courage up and raise my head. The slimeball rolled up in a ball, spinning in mid-air getting faster and faster, he come spinning up to me, he was right in my face. He opened his mouth, it was massive. He roared into my face, pushing my hair in the wind off him. He turned around and flicked his long red spiked tail almost hitting me, he span off into the forest. I couldn't believe my eyes, why has he just left. He had left me here. I lay back on the grass looking up at the blue sky that had appeared. Taking in a deep breath. I knew it was over.

The man and woman walked up to me.

"Louise" the man said in a soft voice. "I have something for you" reaching into his pocket he handed me the last and final key.

"Thank you" I replied looking at the man. "Do I run along?" I asked concerned.

"Do you not want to ask anything?" he asked

"I don't want to be rude sir, but I've had a bit of a rough time in here and all I want to do is get out of here" I replied.

He smiled at me, gave me a pat on the head and sent me on my way. Just as I reached for the handle, he shouted

"you're a true Gorgon girl, we always knew you were, our names are Marley and Leon"

I stopped dead in my tracks.

CHAPTER 8

Marley and Leon

I couldn't believe what he just shouted still holding onto the door handle, I slowly tuned around. "I'm about to meet my parents" I smiled to myself, finally.

"That's right, we are your parents, you've endured the maze of Gubble Gom, you survived the last level with your bravery and selfishness, that's a true Gorgon, we always knew you were" My dad Leon had the softest of voice's you could ever hear, he also spoke slower than we do taking a pause after every word. I looked at him in amazement. I turned to face my mom.

"Hello sweetheart" she smiled at me. She also spoke soft, the love for me in her eyes I could see it twinkling through. She and I really did have the same eyes. I smiled at them both unsure if hugging was a thing in Gubble Gom I just stared at them. I got a feeling I had never had before,

I could stand and stare them all day.

"So come on, let us show you our world" Leon said proud.

We walked towards the door.

"Do you still have the key" Leon asked turning to me.

I nodded and handed over the key, he opened the door and the other side, was a huge village, hundreds of people, well actually Gorgon's. Most of them looked the same as me and you, but others looked different, they were some looking like Nome's like the one from level 1, unusual, dressed ones. Cowboys, Cowgirls.

We started walking down the cobbled path, every man took his hat off to greet my dad and the ladies Curtis. Each one gasping covering their mouths as I walked behind them.

"It's her" I could hear them saying.

Leon turned winked his eye and smiled at me before turning back around to greet everyone. Marley was noticeably quiet; I didn't want to push a conversation out of here so we both walked behind Leon silently. I was busy taking in the scenery, the buildings here were massively tall, some were wonky, some had big bay windows, some had little square windows. We started to walk towards one of the wonky shops 'Gubble Gom's finest Gum' I seen out the coroner of my eye. I tapped Marley,

"May I try some of that gum" I asked politely.

Marley turned to me put her head on my shoulder and replied

"How do I put this to you Lou, there's a lot to learn here first, before you go off trying things, its not like it is on earth, I want to give you everything, but you must learn how to handle yourself first.

I looked at her puzzled guessing it's a no. we walked for what seemed hours when we reached a red brick wall, must have been 10 feet high, there were two purple bricks just off centred

"Are you ready?" Marley asked me.

No idea what I was waiting for I nodded my head gesturing.

"Stand back" Leon asked us both.

He parted his feet, bent his fingers back until they let out a loud crack, and pushed with all his strength on the two purple bricks, a crack appeared to split at the top of the wall carrying on all the way down until the wall was split in two. The bricks started to move until they made a clear doorway for us to walk through. I stood there watching the wall move right in front of my eyes I gasped, and started laughing

"There clearly is a lot to learn here"

Marley and Leon just looked and smiled at me. As I walked through the doorway we were in a huge room, filled with old furniture, sofa, dining tables, cabinets, and hundreds of glassware.

"Take a seat" Marley pointing at the sofa.

I slowly walked over to the sofa running my fingers over all the glassware on my way there.

Marley and Leon followed me over all taking a seat on the sofa.

"Isn't this nice" Marley Smiled.

"Well Louise I don't know where to start, you must have hundreds of questions, but let me start first" Leon Started

"Your mom and me wanted to give you a chance of a normal life, that's the reason you ended up on earth, but you girl you are special, you ended up coming back to us in the end, you're a true Gorgon. Your powers you have are double the strength, you have been given a power no-other Gorgon ever has"

Marley now pacing the living room on edge she abruptly interrupted.

"You don't need to know everything in one day now do you, Leon I think she has heard quite enough" staring at Leon, her pupils growing.

"The girl needs to know!" Leon furiously replied.

They could see me anxiously starting to rub my hands together confused what they were talking about.

"What your dad means, is your special to us and we are glad you are" Marley quickly responded.

I looked over to them both, now sat opposite me.

"So, have you seen me all these years? I know you sent Darcey to watch me, but have you actually seen me?" I asked curiously.

"Of course, we watch you every day, I know everything, we also sent our people to you, the cowboy at the theme park, the girl at your school, I've always been with you, it was me telling you not to take the path you did today, you see here I am a very powerful man, but on earth is a another story, I'm weak I cannot appear, but I'm at your side always" Leon replied.

"And you?" I asked Marley.

Marley looked at Leon as if to wait for him to say whether she can speak or not.

"Go ahead, the girl deserves to know everything" Leon nodded.

"I cannot make it to earth" Marley started

"You see, sometimes you have to make a decision on what is best for you at the time, and sometimes that decision you regret for the rest of your life" she replied trying to hold back the tears.

"Nothing is making sense to me" I cried trying to understand who I was and where I was.

There was a loud knock on the door. Marley and Leon looked at each other in horror.

"You wait here I will back in a minute" Leon said to us.

I looked at Marley, who let out a slight smile and watched Leon leave. I took this time to look at my surroundings, nothing here was very homily, there wasn't any family picture's, no ornaments nothing of any sentimental for 300 years. Leon seemed to have been gone for a while, then I could hear shouting coming from the front door.

"Have you told her yet, she needs to know" this loud voice belting through the living room.

Marley grabbed my arm and started rushing me through to the back of the house.

"What are they talking about?" I shouted. But it was too late. Leon was already standing at the back of the house, with this giant and when I say giant, I mean he was massive! Just his hands where the size of my whole body.

"buzbert" he said holding his hand out for me to shake it.

"You must be Louise" he smiled.

I was just so glad he was a nice guy. I never know here anymore.

"yes" I replied in a shaky voice.

"Well, I'll leave you to it, brickbert, wont fed himself" he smiled.

Marley and Leon followed him to the door. I could hear them talking.

"Tonight Marley, I must know by tonight" Buzbert said.

"We will, I will do it now" Leon replied closing the door shut.

Marley and Leon looked at each other and started walking back to me.

"I suggest you sit down" Leon pointing to the chair.

"Like I was saying earlier, your powers you have, your strength, your speed, your lighting bolt and your.... Never mind," He signed

"The thing is what we need is" he tried to continue
Marley jumping in to save the day.

"The thing is, we need you and your abilities to save our
planet" Marley spat out without hesitation.

"But it's not that simple "Leon shouted out from the background.

"It's very risky for a newbie, and there's a massive consequence if you agree to it, if you say yes you will have to enter the portal of no return, you understand what that means don't you?" he asked.

"But why me" I asked confused

"If you choose to do this, everything will start to make sense, your abilities will become even stronger, you will become stronger, but the choice is yours." Marley replied.

I stared at the floor, not only have I found out my abilities, had to fight my way through levels, I finally meet my parents and now I've been asked to help a planet I don't even know. This night couldn't get any weirder if it tried. I'm still coming to terms with the fact that I have special powers, my parents are 300 years old, there are all sorts of magical creatures here and I've not even explored this place properly. Yet they want me to make a choice.

"If I enter the portal of no return what does that actually mean for me?" I asked concerned.

Marley looked at me and stroked my arm. The first bit of affection I got of my mom; my belly turned.

"We don't know for sure; everyone is different, you see I entered and I could still move around the planets freely, but your mom-she lost the ability to do this, it's a huge decision but we need you now" Leon softly explained.

My heart sank. My mom and dad, I mean Shelly and David what will they do? What if I don't like it here? I might get the chance to go back, but if it goes badly, I will be stuck here regardless.

"How long do I have to decide" I asked "And what is it I need to do? You say you want my help but with what." I finished.

"You see there's this family 'The Cloudy's', they want to take our world, destroy what we have built and make it theirs. We need your strength, courage, and powers to help us defeat them. You don't have much time, we need to train you and make you stronger, I need the decision tonight I'm afraid"

Doesn't give me much time to decided, I began.

"Can I see the portal?" I asked.

Marley and Leon lend me through to the back of the house, through serval doors, down long curved hallways, when we eventually made it to a room. The room wasn't excessively big all four walls was dark brown. To say the rest of this place was so colourful, this room was dingy and empty. I looked around me- there was nothing in here.

"Well, where is it?" I asked curiously.

"Bamboino" shouted Leon.

The wall began to move, behind the brick wall, sat a metal wall. Marley walked up to the metal wall tapped three times, and in an instant the metal wall started spinning and right in the centre a circle appeared, it had blue slime in with a white back light.

"Here is the portal" Leon smiled.

I stared at the portal, without me realising the room had grown twice the size and looming in front of me was this incredible bright light.

"Will it hurt?" I asked scared.

"You won't feel a thing" Smiled Marley.

My head was spinning with all the choices going through my head. I mean it would be so cool if I stayed here,

"Who knows what I could do here, but my family back

home" I cried.

"I'm sorry Lou, but you need to know" Leon said touching my arm.

I walked up to the portal, had a long look through seeing if I can see the exit, as I got closer a huge grey spiked arm reached out. With my heart pumping I lifted my left leg, just reaching the entrance to the portal I replied

"I'm not sure if I can do this"

BOOKS BY THIS AUTHOR

A Witches Tale

Do you believe in witches? Do you enjoy stories that capture the imagination and can take you anywhere you like? Well here is one for you. Julie a house wife bringing her daughter up in a small and safe community but not all is as it seems, being a witch and hiding who you truly are. How long can Julie do this for? When temptation stares her in the face will she be able to overcome her eager of allowing herself to dive into her true meaning.A children's novel based on witches who many centuries ago ruled our world, but now we find they are back and stronger then ever. The queen of witches is waiting for the perfect child to come along. will she get what she wants?

Available on amazon now.

ABOUT THE AUTHOR

Linny Roberts (L.t.r)

I Write to show the world a glimpse into my imagination and i will write till every story in my heart has been told. Even then i will still write because writing isn't something i do, it is me!

Facebook L.T.Rauthor

Printed in Great Britain
by Amazon